My Mercy
Encompasses
All

My Mercy Encompasses All

The Koran's Teachings on Compassion, Peace & Love

Gathered & Introduced by
Reza Shah-Kazemi

WITH A FOREWORD BY WENDELL BERRY

Shoemaker Hoard

Introduction and translations of the Koran copyright © 2007
by Reza Shah-Kazemi
Foreword copyright © 2007 by Wendell Berry

Library of Congress Cataloging-in-Publication Data

Shah-Kazemi, Reza.
My mercy encompasses all: The Koran's teachings on
compassion, peace & love / gathered & introduced by Reza
Shah-Kazemi, foreword by Wendell Berry
p. cm.
ISBN-13: 978-1-59376-144-8
ISBN-10: 1-59376-144-9
1. Koran—Theology. 2. Mercy in the Koran. 3. Love—
Koranic teaching. 4. Peace—Religious aspects—Islam.
I. Title.

BP132.S45 2007
297.1'22521—dc22
2007011837

Cover design by Gerilyn Attebery
Book design by Gerilyn Attebery & Megan Cooney
Printed in the United States of America

Shoemaker ⟨SH⟩ Hoard
www.shoemakerhoard.com

10 9 8 7 6 5 4 3 2 1

Contents ᴈ

Foreword ✌

In 2005, Shoemaker & Hoard published a small anthology, *Blessed Are the Peacemakers,* consisting principally of the Christian Gospels' teachings of peaceability: "Love, Compassion & Forgiveness." And now Reza Shah-Kazemi offers a companion volume assembled from the Koran, *My Mercy Encompasses All.* Between these two small books (the first two, we hope, of a series) we can imagine a sort of ecumenical conversation on the subject of peace. The practical justification for this, as I understand it, is that it is better in all respects for humans to talk to one another than to kill one another.

And so I must begin this foreword by giving my thanks to Reza Shah-Kazemi for his work and care. His selection of verses, along with the introduction and notes, will prove useful to the hoped-for conversation; and it will be clarifying in many ways, I think, to the understanding of the reader. My reading of these pages from Dr. Shah-Kazemi's tradition, not to my surprise, has helped me better to understand my own.

As I read, I thought with some dismay, and some amusement, that the adherents of the Koran and the Bible might be divided into two groups: those who appoint themselves as agents of divine anger, and those who understand themselves as *called to be* agents of divine mercy. As never before, I thought of the unimaginable distance between God's anger and God's love—and of the speed with which Christians sometimes move from God's presumed anger at other people to his presumptive love for themselves.

To think of oneself as an agent of God's anger is exceedingly attractive; perhaps this is the temptation that the Lord's Prayer appeals to God not to lead us into. There are certain intense pleasures in anger, especially if one's own anger can be presumed to coincide with God's, and also in the use of an angry self-righteousness as a standard by which to condemn other people. This is a pleasure necessarily founded on the shallowest sort of self-knowledge. There is much comedy in this (as Shakespeare, for one, knew well), and also great tragedy. It is evidently possible to indulge one's own anger, justifying it as God's, and relying on God's mercy hereafter—but that seems to bet against great odds, and with hell to pay here and now for a lot of people. For those who appoint themselves agents of God's anger, there can be only division and strife until the end of time.

To take up, by contrast, the agency of God's mercy seems to involve one in a labor of self-knowledge and then knowledge of others that is endlessly humbling. This perhaps is a comedy of another kind: We ourselves are in need of those things we are called upon to give to others: compassion, forgiveness, mercy. And unless we give them, we cannot receive them. God's mercy is of interest to us only in the light of our recognition of our need for it. Those who accept the agency of God's mercy, understanding their own need for it as the index of the need of others, must forbear their anger and talk together ("hold discourse" in the language of Dr. Shah-Kazemi's translation) until the end of time, for God's mercy is a mystery never to be fully known or enacted by humans.

—*Wendell Berry*

Introduction ❧

I F THE CONCEPT OF UNITY dominates the mind, it is the principle of compassion that governs the heart in Islam. Compassion is to oneness what radiance is to the sun: It is through compassion that the oneness of God most brilliantly shines forth and reveals its fundamental nature. Since compassion stems from oneness, it not only radiates, it also integrates; it exerts a merciful attraction upon all outward multiplicity: "My Mercy encompasses all things" (7:156).

On the human plane, "compassion"—the capacity to feel and be "with" *(com)* the other in their "suffering" *(passio)*—expresses not just human sentiment but also spiritual presentiment; compassion arises first and foremost out of one's innate sense of the interconnected oneness of all human beings. Speaking to the whole of humanity, the Koran declares: "Your creation, and your resurrection, is but as a single soul" (31:28). The boundaries separating oneself from all others are rendered transparent in the light of the intrinsic oneness of humanity. And this unity of humanity is itself a reflection of the oneness of God.

The doctrine of the oneness of God is given expression in the first testimony of Islam: *la ilaha illa'Llah*, no divinity but God. This oneness is conceived in two complementary modes: It is both utterly remote, exclusive, transcending all things, and inescapably intimate, inclusive, immanently pervading all things. On the one hand, "There is nothing like Him"; and on the other, God is "closer to man than his jugular vein." It is in terms of this relationship of intimacy, proximity, inclusiveness, and ultimately, identity that the principle of compassion emerges most clearly. Among the classical ninety-nine "Most Beautiful Names" of God, which are based on how the divine Reality describes itself in the Koran, we find such names as "the All-Encompassing," "the Infinitely Vast" *(al-Muhit; al-Wasi')*: the inclusive oneness of God, by virtue of which nothing whatsoever escapes from the divine presence, is inseparable from the Mercy of God, from which, likewise, nothing whatsoever can escape: "My Mercy encompasses all things."

The divine Names most clearly associated with mercy and compassion are given in the formula by which every significant act in Islam is consecrated, and with which every chapter of the Koran begins,[1] the formula known as the *basmala:* "In the Name of God, the Compassionate, the Merciful" *(bismi'Llahi r-Rahmani r-Rahim).* The two Names, *al-Rahman* and *al-Rahim,* share the same root *(r-h-m),* and both express *rahma,* the meaning of which comprises the qualities of compassion, mercy, forgiveness, loving goodness. "Call upon *Allah* or call upon *al-Rahman,*" the Koran tells us, expressing the quasi-equivalence between "the Compassionate" and God as such, thereby indicating the defining characteristic or "identity" of the ineffable One, "whichever of these two [Names] you call upon, unto Him belong the most beautiful Names" (17:110).

Given the fact that among the divine Names one also finds "the Almighty," "the Avenger,"

---

1. All, that is, with the exception of one, Chapter 9. There are 114 chapters in the Koran, and in fact the formula does appear 114 times in the text, as it is also given once in the middle of Chapter 27 (verse 30), where the story of Solomon and Sheba is recounted.

and other Names expressive of divine rigor, it is of great significance that the formula of consecration contains a repetition of the theme of mercy; one might have thought it more "logical" or balanced to include a name of rigor in this definitive consecration describing the essential nature of the "God" in whose name one begins everything, and thus have something like: "In the Name of God, the Compassionate, the Powerful." The very fact that two Names of Mercy are given in this formula, which inaugurates the revelation and consecrates every act of significance for the Muslim, allows one to see that the essential nature of ultimate Reality is compassionate and merciful, these two qualities being expressive of the overflow of infinite love.

In the spiritual tradition of Islam, great stress is placed on love as being the fountainhead of creation. "I was a hidden treasure," God declares, "and I loved to be known, so I created the world."[2] The Names of Mercy,

---

2. This is a *hadith qudsi,* that is, a saying in which God speaks through the tongue of the Prophet. God is therefore the speaker, but this kind of saying is not part of the Koran. Although the majority of formal scholars of Islam regard this particular saying as lacking a strong chain of narrators, they nonetheless accept its meaning, which is confirmed by many other sayings and verses of the Koran. For the spiritual authorities of Islam, this saying is of fundamental importance, providing a rich source of mystical reflection.

al-Rahman and *al-Rahim,* give voice to this creative impulse of divine love, and they are both related to the word *rahm,* which means "womb." Here one glimpses another mystery of the all-embracing oneness of mercy: Just as the womb entirely envelops the embryo growing within it, the divine "matrix" of compassion contains and nourishes the whole corpus of existence unfolding within itself. The qualities of divine anger are not being denied in this perspective; rather, they are seen as the inevitable consequences of human sin. The latter is by definition limited and relative, so the divine qualities elicited by relativity cannot be placed on the same level as those that flow forth from the very nature of the Absolute. Thus we are told not only that "My Mercy encompasses all things" but also that "My Mercy takes precedence over My Anger."[3] On the one hand, there is the rigorous restoration of an equilibrium ruptured by the sins of relative beings; on the other, the merciful reintegration of purified souls within the beatific nature of the Absolute.

---

3. This is another *hadith qudsi,* but this time one strongly authenticated by the formal scholars as well as by the spiritual figures of Islam. It is recorded in the most authoritative compilations of prophetic sayings, such as those of Bukhari and Muslim.

The Koran describes the divine Mercy in a manner that is as inspiring as it is overwhelming: God's love is infinite and thus His Mercy is given to us "beyond all reckoning," beyond anything "deserved" by us; this is a key dimension of the spiritual justice of God: "Whoever comes [before God] with a good deed will receive ten like it; but whoever comes [before God] with an evil deed will only be requited with its like; and no injustice will be done to them" (6:160). Another revealing aspect of the relationship between the divine Mercy and the divine Anger is implicit at the end of the very first chapter of the Koran, called *al-Fatiha* (The Opening), which is recited several times each day as the foundation of the canonical prayers of every Muslim:

In the Name of God, the Compassionate, the Merciful

Praise be to God, Lord of all the worlds,

The Compassionate, the Merciful,

Lord of the Day of Judgment,

Thee alone we worship, and from Thee alone we seek help,

Guide us along the straight path,

The path of those Thou hast blessed

Not of those upon whom is anger, nor of those who go astray.

It is to be noted that God's Anger is not specifically mentioned in the last verse; it is those who are the objects of anger, those who elicit anger that are referred to; the subject of the anger can be either God or the soul or both, the one being an aspect of the other. On the contrary, the divine Mercy is stressed again and again, and the sole *act* directly attributed to God in this prayer is blessing: The Muslim seeks to be guided along the straight path, the path of those whom God has *blessed*. One is drawn into the mystery expressed more directly in this verse: "Whatever good comes to you is from God, and whatever evil comes to you is from your own soul" (4:79). And, more explicitly: "We have tied every man's augury to his own neck, and We shall bring forth for him on the Day of Judgment a book that he will find open wide. [It will be said to him:] Read your book. Your own soul suffices this day unto you as a reckoner" (17:13).

In the light of these and several other verses, one is able to move from an anthropomorphic conception of divine Anger to an ontological one: Rather than picture God as some gigantic man in the sky who punishes and forgives at will, one is drawn into the mysterious depths of the true nature of being. Ruptures in being must needs be rectified, not by some arbitrary act by a capricious individual, but by the immutable principles of justice and peace, truth and love, principles of which the ultimate nature of Reality is woven. In the mystical tradition of Islam it is said that the "Anger of God" is nothing but the extrinsic consequence of the lack of the soul's receptivity to the mercy that eternally radiates from the very nature of being. This mercy is calling out to the soul in every moment, and it is for the soul but to respond in order to be given beatific life in the Real: "O you who believe, respond to God and the Messenger when He invites you to that which gives you life" (8:24).

However much the acts and attitudes of a few misguided individuals in our times may have obscured the compassion that flows forth from the very nature of the Islamic way, it remains an incontrovertible fact that mercy predominates over anger, both as regards the divine nature and within the human realm. If God describes His Anger as being subordinated to His Mercy, the same principial priority must obtain within the human soul. The human participation in the divine quality of compassion is made crystal clear in the Koran. Whenever God is described in terms of compassion and peace and love, it is always implied that the soul is being called upon to assimilate these qualities: Those Names and qualities that characterize God must also characterize man—mutatis mutandis; what is true of God in absolute mode must be true of man in relative mode. The divine qualities are thus to be viewed as the source and very substance of human virtues: No divinity but God comes to imply that there is no human virtue that is not a reflection of a divine quality.

There is another aspect of the human participation in divine Mercy that relates to the function of the Prophet Muhammad: For if God is continuously described as being compassionate and merciful, so, too, is the Prophet, who stands forth as the exemplar par excellence for the whole of humanity. "We sent you not [O Prophet] except as a mercy for all the worlds" (21:107). If the Prophet is, in his very being as well as in his actions, nothing but a "mercy" unto all beings, the same ought to be said of every Muslim who seeks to be true to the Koranic injunction to model his life totally upon the character of the Prophet: "Truly you have in the Messenger of God a beautiful example, for whosoever places his hope in God and the Last Day, and who remembers God much." And, even more explicitly: "If you love God," the Prophet is told to declare to the believers, "then follow me; God will love you and forgive you your sins. God is Forgiving, Merciful" (3:31).

To follow the Prophet's example is to be, first and foremost, a "mercy" to all the worlds, in the measure of one's own possibilities, within the sphere of one's own "world." All the other aspects of following the Prophet's example are to be appreciated in the light of this fundamental—one might say, cosmological—function of radiating that Mercy that is at one with the very nature of God. To love God is to love His Love, which is expressed in myriad forms of creative manifestation, guiding revelation, and merciful reintegration. All three principles are manifested in the Prophet as the "perfect man" *(al-insan al-kamil):* It is thus that love of God is inseparable from the emulation of the Prophet, he who is not just "the Messenger of God" but also the very embodiment herebelow of the reflected Mercy of God on high.

It has often been said that Islam is a synthesis of its two sister-religions in the Abrahamic family of Semitic monotheism. Indeed, one will find in the Koran passages that evoke the legal injunctions of Deuteronomy, the lyrical supplications of the Psalms of David, and the sermons of Jesus in the Gospels. But the Koran is much more than simply a synthesis of its Semitic predecessors. It is also, as it says of itself, a *Musaddiq,* that is, a "confirmation" of all revelation that preceded it, and a *Muhaymin* (protector) of all scriptures (see 5:48). Thus, one is entitled to regard the Koran as a divine seal on the whole cycle of prophetic revelation, confirming and protecting all true revelations, whatever the form and wherever the place and whenever the time. The all-encompassing nature of the Koranic view of religion can be seen in several verses. For example: "Truly those who believe, and the Jews, and the Christians and the Sabeans—whosoever believes in God and the Day of Judgment, and acts virtuously will receive their reward from their Lord; no fear or grief will befall them" (2:62).

The following verse adds a dimension of concrete actuality to the claim of the Koran to be a protector of all revelations: "Permission [to fight back] is granted to those who are being fought, for they have been wronged . . . those who have been expelled from their homes unjustly, only because they said: 'Our Lord is God.' Had God not driven back some people by means of others, then monasteries, churches, synagogues, and mosques—places where the Name of God is oft-invoked—would assuredly have been destroyed" (22:39–40). This verse is regarded by most commentators on the Koran as the very first to be revealed in relation to warfare and thus makes absolutely clear two fundamental principles: first, that Muslims are to fight only in self-defense; and second, the Muslims are to fight in defense of *all* believers and their places of worship. The purpose of warfare is to establish peace, and this peace is, evidently, supposed to govern relations between all believers. All the verses of the Koran cited by "jihadists" in their vain effort to justify the indiscriminate murder of non-Muslims are to be seen in the light of these two fundamental principles.[4]

---

4. See D. Dakake, "The Myth of a Militant Islam," in J. Lumbard (ed.), *Islam, Fundamentalism and the Betrayal of Tradition* (Bloomington: World Wisdom, 2004), especially pp. 3–16, where a careful analysis is given of the verses cited out of context and distorted beyond recognition by the jihadists.

The formal religion of Islam is conceived as the final articulation of the "primordial religion" *(din al-fitra)*, which manifests at the core of every divine revelation; it is in this light that the following words addressed to the Prophet should be understood: "Naught was said to you but what was said to the Messengers who came before you" (41:43). The core or essence of revelation is immutable and universal, whatever be the diverse forms by which it is clothed; these forms are diverse because of the diversity of mankind: "And of His signs is the creation of the heavens and the earth, and the diversity of your languages and your colors" (30:22); and also: "O mankind, We have indeed created you as male and female, and made you as nations and tribes that you might come to know one another" (49:13). It is on account of this formal diversity that religious revelation perforce assumes forms that are diverse and sometimes apparently contradictory. But this formal diversity is inescapable, inasmuch as "We never sent a messenger but with the language of his folk" (14:4).

From the formal, theological point of view, what is in question here is a rather superficial difference of language behind which there lies an identical semantic content of the one and only message; from the spiritual point of view, however, this very diversity of formal revelation is grasped as an expression of pure mercy.[5] The divine self-disclosure takes on multiple forms as a compassionate means of reaching out to humanity in terms that are intelligible to people of all ethnic, racial, and cultural backgrounds. If God's Mercy "encompasses all things," so too must His revealed guidance embrace all peoples: "And for every community there is a messenger" (10:47).

The peace and harmony that Islam envisages—and so often in its history witnessed—as governing the relations between adherents of different faiths is itself the fruit of this conception of the compassion inherent in the dazzling diversity and all-encompassing universality of divine self-revelation. One cannot begin to appreciate the extraordinary—indeed unparalleled—

---

5. It is perhaps in the corpus of the renowned Sufi Ibn Arabi (d. 1240) that the principle of mercy is given the most profound treatment in the Islamic intellectual tradition. See W. C. Chittick, *The Sufi Path of Knowledge* (New York: SUNY, 1989); T. Izutsu, *Sufism and Taoism* (Berkeley: University of California Press, 1983), especially chap. 9, "Ontological Mercy," pp. 116–140; and H. Corbin, *Creative Imagination in the Sufism of Ibn Arabi,* trans. R. Mannheim (Princeton: Princeton University Press, 1969), especially chap. 1, "Divine Passion and Compassion," pp. 105–135.

record of religious tolerance in the history of Islam without taking account of this principle of divine compassion expressing itself in diverse forms. One is thus very far from a sentimental "anything goes" type of mentality; tolerance flows forth in Islam as a principled, compassionate response to the divine source of the revelation lying at the root of the religions of "the Other."[6]

However, it may well be asked whether such a subtle view of divine Mercy is but the fruit of sophisticated speculation by the refined few; to what extent does such a perspective influence the actual conduct of Muslims in the past or in the present? Although this book is not the place to answer this question in detail, one can address the relationship between Koranic theory and Muslim practice, however briefly, and let some of the facts speak for themselves. Two examples can be given here, one drawn from the Middle Ages, the other from our own times. First, let us listen to the account given by the Christian chronicler Ernoul of the conduct of Saladin after his momentous

---

6. See Reza Shah-Kazemi, *The Other in the Light of the One: The Universality of the Qur'an and Interfaith Dialogue* (Cambridge: Islamic Texts Society, 2006), for discussion of this theme.

victory over the Christian Crusader kingdom
of Jerusalem in 1187:

> Then I shall tell you of the great courtesy
> which Saladin showed to the wives and
> daughters of knights, who had fled to Jeru-
> salem when their lords were killed or made
> prisoners in battle. When these ladies were
> ransomed and had come forth from Jerusa-
> lem, they assembled and went before Sala-
> din crying mercy. When Saladin saw them
> he asked who they were and what they
> sought. And it was told him that they were
> the dames and damsels of knights who
> had been taken or killed in battle. Then
> he asked what they wished, and they an-
> swered for God's sake have pity on them;
> for the husbands of some were in prison,
> and of others were dead, and they had lost
> their lands, and in the name of God let him
> counsel and help them. When Saladin saw
> them weeping he had great compassion for
> them, and wept himself for pity. And he
> bade the ladies whose husbands were alive
> to tell him where they were captives, and
> as soon as he could go to the prisons he
> would set them free. And all were released
> wherever they were found. After that he
> commanded that to the dames and dam-
> sels whose lords were dead there should
> be handsomely distributed from his own
> treasure, to some more and others less, ac-
> cording to their estate. And he gave them
> so much that they gave praise to God and

published abroad the kindness and honour which Saladin had done to them.[7]

Saladin's compassion at this defining moment of world history will always be contrasted with the barbaric sacking of the city and indiscriminate murder of its inhabitants by the Christian Crusaders in 1099. His lesson of mercy has been immortalized in the words of his biographer, Stanley Lane-Poole:

> One recalls the savage conquest by the first Crusaders in 1099, when Godfrey and Tancred rode through streets choked with the dead and the dying, when defenceless Moslems were tortured, burnt, and shot down in cold blood on the towers and roof of the Temple, when the blood of wanton massacre defiled

---

7. Quoted in Stanley Lane-Poole, *Saladin and the Fall of the Kingdom of Jerusalem* (Beirut: Khayats Oriental Reprints, 1964; originally published in London, 1898), pp. 232–233. Saladin was, of course, renowned throughout the Middle Ages and down to our own times as the very epitome of chivalry. The influence of the knightly ideal of Islam on Western Christendom has been clearly discerned by observers. Simonde de Sismondi, writing in the early nineteenth century, asserts that key themes in Muslim culture and Arabic literature provided one source of "that tenderness and delicacy of sentiment and that reverential awe of women . . . which have operated so powerfully on our chivalrous feelings." *Histoire de la littérature du Midi de l'Europe*, quoted in R. Boase, *The Origin and Meaning of Courtly Love* (Manchester: Manchester University Press, 1977), p. 20.

the honour of Christendom and stained the scene where once the gospel of love and mercy had been preached. "Blessed are the merciful, for they shall obtain mercy" was a forgotten beatitude when the Christians made shambles of the Holy City. Fortunate were the merciless, for they obtained mercy at the hands of the Moslem Sultan. . . . If the taking of Jerusalem were the only fact known about Saladin, it were enough to prove him the most chivalrous and great-hearted conqueror of his own, and perhaps of any, age.[8]

Coming closer to our own times, let us take careful note of the theme of Koranic mercy that permeates the response of one leading Bosnian intellectual and former vice president of the country, Professor Rusmir Mahmutćehajić, to the atrocities perpetrated against the Bosnian Muslims by the Serbs in the genocide of the 1990s.

> More than a thousand of their *masdjids* [mosques] have been destroyed, over a hundred and fifty thousand people killed, over fifty thousand women and girls raped,

---

8. Lane-Poole, *Saladin and the Fall of the Kingdom of Jerusalem*, pp. 233–234. For more examples of such principles in action, see Reza Shah-Kazemi, "From the Spirituality of Jihad to the Ideology of Jihadism," *Seasons: Semiannual Journal of the Zaytuna Institute* 2, no. 2 (Spring–Summer Reflections, 2005), pp. 45–68.

and more than a million people expelled from their homes. The dark forces of human evil have touched every aspect of their existence—hence the danger of their becoming so radicalised by suffering that they take on the nature of the perpetrators. The other choice is to realise the true meaning of the first image, the *masdjid*, and to hold by it, while facing the immediate need to confront, analyse and identify this evil. The image of the *masdjid*, and the fact of the killings, offer a spectrum of possibilities, ranging from the highest—the Vertical Path—to the lowest—descent into rage.[9]

The response of Mahmutćehajić? To follow the command of the Koran:

> The good deed and the evil deed are not equal. Repel [evil] with that which is most beautiful in goodness, and then [it can happen that] your enemy will be like a dear friend. But none is granted [such a capacity to respond to evil] except those who are patient; and none is granted it except those who have been blessed with immense good fortune. (41:34–35)

---

9. Rusmir Mahmutćehajić, *Bosnia the Good: Tolerance and Tradition,* trans. Marina Bowder (Budapest: Central European University Press, 2000), p. 144.

The magnanimous—indeed extraordinarily heroic—capacity to forgive is here clearly linked to the deepest meaning of the term *islam,* all too often read simply as a label to be applied to those who are Muslims. When translated literally, it is rendered simply as "submission" or "surrender." In Arabic, however, this term is inextricably tied to the notion of peace, *salam,* the two words sharing a common root. The one who "submits" entirely to God is one who attains the deepest peace, for the attunement to divine reality generated by heartfelt submission opens one's soul to the influx of the infinite peace and imperturbable serenity of God; also implied in the root of this word is salvation, being saved from punishment in the Hereafter and, more subtly, from the assaults of egotistic impulse in the herebelow. Thus, whenever one reads or hears the word *islam* and the description *Muslim,* one should always have in mind the principles of peace and salvation, as well as submission and surrender. When reading the Koran, every instance of these two key terms should evoke the profound peace that arises out of submission to God and that does so in proportion to the sincerity of that submission.

A similar point needs to be made in relation to the terms *iman* (faith) and *mu'min* (believer): The basic meaning of these two words is that of security. When applied to the divine reality, the name *al-Mu'min* comes to mean "He who gives security, safety," whereas applied to human beings, it is more normally translated as "believer." However, it is possible to see the human quality of "faith" participating directly in the divine function of "making safe": One enters that impregnable refuge of divine protection in the very measure in which one's faith is sincere and profound. One needs to make analogous remarks about the term *ihsan,* the third of this ternary of terms—*islam, iman, ihsan*—that is so central in the religious lexicon of Islam. Normally translated as "virtue," "goodness," the root meaning of the word is "beauty," and it is thus that beauty of soul is the very definition of good character in the Muslim ethical worldview. Good action is intrinsically beautiful, evil being intrinsically ugly. Although we cannot do justice to all the instances in the Koran where this combination of beauty and virtue is implied in the use of this term, a few examples will be given in the selections.

One can envisage the following objection to a compilation of this nature: The selected verses show only one side of the Koranic message, and by ignoring the severe and wrathful side, a misleading picture is being presented. Many both within and without the Islamic faith would make such an objection, and it is of course a valid one, to a certain extent. The Koran is to be taken as a totality, and the balance between "the promise" and "the threat" *(al-wa'd wa al-wa'id),* between hope and fear, between gentleness and rigor, is continually maintained throughout the text. An over-accentuation on the one element to the detriment of the other distorts the integrity of the message and diminishes the psychological impact of the text as a whole upon the soul. But this is precisely what has been done in our times, in the very opposite direction: The wrathful, severe side of Islamic teachings has been presented in a unilateral manner, so that, on an apparently Koranic foundation, a theology of hate has been formulated that serves as a façade behind which a blatantly un-Islamic political ideology can operate.

It is for this reason that works such as this one, which admittedly presents only one side of the picture—the peaceful, loving, and compassionate side—are so badly needed in our times. It is our hope and prayer that the present selection of verses will help to draw attention to the absolute centrality of the principles of compassion and mercy, peace and love in the Koranic worldview. If divine Mercy takes precedence over divine Anger, it is because "My Mercy encompasses all things" and because God "has prescribed mercy for Himself" (6:12). Mercy will indeed have the last word.

Selections from the Koran ❧

୬୬ Note on the Translation ୬୬

I HAVE TRANSLATED THESE Koranic verses
making use, principally, of what is still con-
sidered by many to be the best available com-
plete English translation of the Koran, that
of Muhammad Marmaduke Pickthall. The
translations of the following scholars were
also consulted: Abdallah Yusuf Ali, A. J. Arberry, Muhammad Asad, M. A. S. Abdel
Haleem, N. J. Dawood, and Muhammad
Ali. Despite opting for contemporary rather
than classical English, I have made occasional
use of the old English "thee/thou" forms
of the second person singular, particularly
when God is being addressed. Ellipses in the
Arabic text are filled in with words given in
square brackets.

—*Reza Shah-Kazemi*

1. That is, after his act of disobedience, eating fruit from the forbidden tree. That is described in the preceding verses, 2:30–36. The point to be stressed here is that the divine Mercy is manifest immediately after the fall of Adam, both in terms of acceptance of his repentance and in the form of revealed guidance, both for Adam himself and for all human communities to come in the wake of his fall from grace.

2. The exclusivism to which all religious believers are prone is here explicitly criticized. The Muslims are also warned against the "vanity" of exclusivism: They are told, "It will not be in accordance with your desires, nor with the desires of the People of the Book [Jews and Christians]: whoever does evil will be requited for it . . . and whoever does good works, male or female, and is a believer, such will enter Paradise and they will not be wronged the dint of a date-stone" (4:123–124). One is saved not because of some formal religious affiliation or the other, but by the grace of God, on the one hand, and faith and virtue, on the other. See the introduction for discussion of the relationship between the all-inclusive compassion of God and the all-embracing conception of revelation and salvation, and for citation of 2:62, which unequivocally promises salvation not just to the Jews, Christians, and Sabeans, but to "whosoever believes in God and the Day of Judgment, and acts virtuously."

Then[1] Adam received words of mercy from his Lord, and He relented towards him. Truly, He is the Relenting, the Merciful. We said: "Get down from here, altogether; but when guidance comes to you from Me, as it assuredly will, whoever follows My guidance shall not fear, neither shall they grieve."

2:111–112

They say: "None enters Paradise except a Jew or a Christian." These are their vain desires. Say: "Bring your proof if you speak the truth." Nay, but whoever submits his entire being to God, and he is virtuous, his reward is with his Lord; [such persons] shall not fear, neither shall they grieve.[2]

2:153–155

O believers, seek help in patience and in prayer. Truly God is ever with the patient. And say not regarding those who have been slain in the cause of God: "They are dead." Nay, they are alive, but you perceive it not. And We surely shall try you by means of fear and hunger, loss of wealth and lives and harvest. But give good tidings to the patient,

3. The term translated here as "piety" is *al-birr,* which could also be translated as "righteousness," "goodness," and/or "sincerity." The righteousness in question is heartfelt and sincere, flowing from intimate contact with, or sincere faith in, the supreme source of goodness, the sovereign Good, God as such: One of the Names of God is related to the same root as this word, *al-Barr,* "the Good/Benevolent" (see 52:28). It should be remembered that the Latin root of the word *benevolent* relates to "goodwill" (*bene* = good; *velle* = to wish). This sincere piety is contrasted with the superficial attitude of self-righteousness or sanctimoniousness that equates the formal act of prayer with piety; "turning your faces to the East or the West" in your formal prayers does not qualify one as truly pious. Such prayer is an essential but not sufficient condition of piety; one must "observe the prayer" but one must also conform inwardly and outwardly to the sovereign Good to whom the prayers are directed—whence the stress on all the benevolent actions and virtues described in the rest of the verse.

4. By this is meant all revelations by God to humankind. As discussed in the introduction, the Koran refers to itself as a "confirmer and preserver" of all scriptural revelations prior to the Koran; see 5:48. A fundamental tenet of the Islamic credo is belief in all revelations: The Muslims are those who "believe in God, and His angels, and His Scriptures, and His messengers; [they say:] 'We make no distinction between any of His messengers'" (2:285).

5. An alternative translation: "despite loving their wealth."

6. One of the Names of God is *al-Qarib,* "the Near."

those who say, when afflicted by adversity:
"We belong to God, and verily unto Him are
we ever returning." These are the ones upon
whom there are blessings from their Lord,
and mercy—these are the rightly guided.

2:177

Piety is not turning your faces to the East or
the West;[3] rather, piety is [expressed by] those
who believe in God and the Last Day, and in
the angels, the Scripture,[4] and the prophets;
and who spend their wealth—for the love of
God[5]—upon close relatives, orphans, the needy,
wayfarers, beggars, and upon freeing [those in
slavery]; and who observe the prayers and pay
the alms tax; and who keep whatever promises
they make; and who are patient in times of trib-
ulation, adversity, and distress. These are the
sincere, and these are the God-fearing.

2:186

And when my servants ask you about Me:
verily I am near;[6] I answer the prayer of the
suppliant when he calls upon Me. So let them
answer Me, and believe in Me, that they might
be led aright.

7. As Muhammad Asad notes, this verse is one of several that "lay down unequivocally that only self-defense (in the widest sense of the word) makes war permissible for Muslims. Most of the commentators [on the Koran] agree, in that the expression *la ta'tadu* signifies, in this context, 'do not commit aggression'; while by *al-mu'tadin*, 'those who commit aggression' are meant." M. Asad, *The Message of the Qur'an* (Bristol: Book Foundation, 2003), vol. 1, p. 51, n. 167. See also verses 4:90, 22:39, 60:8, et passim, where the essentially defensive nature of war in Islam is stressed.

8. This principle of proportionate retaliation concerns the harsh exigencies of the political and military domains; however, on the moral and spiritual planes, it is the principle of forgiveness that prevails, as is stressed in so many of the verses cited here. The principle of retaliation is also to be nuanced in the light of the following verse: "If you respond [to any opposition] then respond in a proportionate manner, but if you bear [it] patiently, that is better" (16:126, see below).

9. This translates *Halim*, one of the divine Names. As a human attribute, the gentleness in question is to be understood in relation to the qualities of forbearance and patience that stem from self-dominion, and the graciousness and serenity that flow from true wisdom—all of which are connoted by the Arabic term *hilm*. The original meaning of the word *gentle* (whence today's "gentleman") came closer to what is evoked by the term *hilm*, as is suggested by Shakespeare in the following line uttered by the Lord Chamberlain in *Henry VIII*: "You bear a gentle mind, and heavenly blessings follow such creatures" (Act 2, Scene 3). Likewise, Dante brings out the aspects of grace and nobility inherent in the Latin root of the word when he writes in his *Vita Nuova*: "Amore e'l cor gentil sono una cosa" (Love and a gentle heart are but one and the same thing).

2:190

Fight in the cause of God those who wage war against you, but do not commit aggression. Truly, God loves not aggressors.[7]

2:194

. . . A sacred month for a sacred month: violation of sanctity [requires] proportionate retribution. So if anyone commits aggression against you, then attack him as he attacked you; but be mindful of God, and know that God is always with those who are mindful of Him.[8]

2:256

There is no compulsion in religion.

2:262–263

Those who spend their wealth in the cause of God—and who do not draw attention to their benevolence or utter hurtful words after having spent thus—their reward is with their Lord, they shall not fear, neither shall they grieve. A kind word with forgiveness is better than charity followed by hurtfulness. And God is Self-Sufficient, Gentle.[9]

2:268

The devil promises you destitution and orders foul deeds, whereas God promises you His forgiveness and overflowing grace.

2:271

If you give charity openly, that is good; but if you hide it, while bestowing it upon those in need, that is better for you.

3:31

Say [O Muhammad]: If you love God, follow me; God will love you and forgive you your sins. God is Forgiving, Merciful.

3:76, 92

Nay, but whoever fulfills his trust and is pious —God indeed loves those who are pious.

. . . You will not attain piety until you give to others what you cherish for yourselves.

3:133–136

And hasten to the forgiveness of your Lord, and to a Garden as vast as the heavens and the

10. "Those who radiate through beautiful virtue" translates
al-muhsinin, normally rendered as "the virtuous." See
the discussion of the term *ihsan* in the Introduction.

earth which is prepared for the pious—those who give to others in times of ease and adversity; those who control their anger and are forgiving towards others—and God loves those who radiate through beautiful virtue;[10] those who, when they commit a foul deed or wrong themselves, remember God and seek forgiveness of their sins—and who forgives sins but God?; those who do not knowingly persist in such deeds. These are the ones whose reward is forgiveness from their Lord, and Gardens beneath which rivers flow, to abide therein forever—how excellent is the reward of those who strive!

3:159

It was through the mercy of God that you [O Prophet] were gentle with them. For if you had been harsh and hard-hearted they would have fled from you. So pardon them, and pray that they be forgiven; and consult with them in public affairs. . . .

4:31

If you avoid the major sins which are prohibited to you, then We will efface your evil deeds, and have you enter a noble abode.

4:64

. . . If, when they had wronged themselves, they had but come to you [O Prophet], and asked forgiveness of God, and if the Messenger had prayed for them to be forgiven, they would assuredly have found God to be ever-pardoning, merciful.

4:90

. . . If they [the adversaries of the Muslims] leave you alone, and do not wage war against you, and offer you peace, then God does not allow you to fight them.

4:110

Whoever does evil, or wrongs himself, then seeks the forgiveness of God, will find God Forgiving, Merciful.

4:114

No good comes from much of their private discussions, except [from] those who enjoin charity, kindness, or peace-making among people. And We shall bestow a tremendous reward upon whoever does this, seeking the good pleasure of God.

11. That is, if a person commits the charitable act of forgoing his legal right to retaliation, it will serve as an atonement, in the eyes of God, for him. See Exodus 21:23–25 and Leviticus 24:19–21 for the laws being referred to here. In this case, as in so many other instances, one sees the way in which the Koranic teaching is a synthesis of the legal aspect of Jewish scripture and the spiritual aspect of the Christic message. The law of retaliation must govern the social order, whereas the spirit of forgiveness must infuse the soul of the individual and thus, on occasion, take precedence over the law.

4:147

Why should God punish you, if you are grateful to Him, and believe?

5:8

O you who believe, be steadfast and upright
for God, bearing witness with justice, and
never let hatred of a people cause you to deal
unjustly with them. Be just—that is closest to
piety . . .

5:32

. . . Whoever saves the life of one human being, it shall be as if he had saved the whole of
humankind . . .

5:44–45

Truly We revealed the Torah—wherein is guidance and light—by which the prophets who
submitted judged the Jews, as did the rabbis
and the priests. . . . In the Torah We prescribed
for them a life for a life, an eye for an eye, a
nose for a nose, an ear for an ear, a tooth for a
tooth, and for a wound, proportionate retaliation. But whoever forgoes this, as an act of
charity, it will be an atonement for him.[11]

12. This remarkable verse—furnishing us with the clear-
est possible scriptural explanation of the reason for religious diversity—teaches us that each of the religions
is rooted in divine revelation and is thus to be revered
and not just tolerated. Peaceful coexistence with adherents of other faiths, on the basis of authentic respect,
is the natural consequence of this fundamental teaching
of the Koran. See Reza Shah-Kazemi, *The Other in the
Light of the One: The Universality of the Qur'an and
Interfaith Dialogue* (Cambridge: Islamic Texts Society,
2006), for further discussion.

5:48

And We have revealed unto you the Scripture
with the Truth, confirming what came before
it of Scripture and as a guardian over it. . . .
For each We have appointed a Law and a Way.
And had God willed, He could have made you
one community. But [He made you as you are]
so that He might test you by means of that
which He has given you. So vie one with another in virtue. Unto God you will all return,
and He will inform you about that over which
you had differences.[12]

5:82

You will surely find that, of all people, the
ones who are nearest in love to those who believe [in the revelation of the Koran] are those
who say: "We are Christians." That is because
there are among them priests and monks, and
because they are not proud. When they hear
that which has been revealed to the Prophet,
you see their eyes overflow with tears, in recognition of its truth. . . .

13. The Arabic here uses the word *kataba*, "he wrote," the implication being: wrote a law, thus making incumbent, so that one could also translate this phrase as "He has made mercy incumbent upon Himself"; this image of writing a law for oneself can be seen as a graphic metaphor for expressing the metaphysical truth that mercy is, as it were, "inscribed" or embedded in the very nature of ultimate reality. No other quality of God is described in this manner, thus one is compelled to see once again the predominance of mercy within the divine nature and, by extension, throughout the created realm.

14. See also 28:84 for the same principle. The lack of common measure between the reward for good and the recompense of evil described here is one concrete—or "mathematical"—expression of the principial predominance of mercy and goodness over all other qualities. Since God has "prescribed mercy for Himself," the reward for good must needs outweigh the recompense of evil.

6:12

Say: Unto whom belongs whatever is in the heavens and the earth? Say: unto God. He has prescribed[13] mercy for Himself . . .

6:54

And when those who believe in Our revelations come to you, say: Peace be with you; your Lord has prescribed mercy for Himself, so that whoever among you does evil in ignorance, and then repents afterwards, and makes amends—[will find that] God is indeed Forgiving, Merciful.

6:160

Whoever comes [before God] with a good deed will receive ten like it; but whoever comes [before God] with an evil deed will only be requited with its like; and no injustice will be done to them.[14]

7:156

. . . And My Mercy encompasses all things.

15. These are the words of Shu'ayb (called Jethro in the Old Testament), father-in-law of Moses, addressed to his people, the folk of Midian. The source of God's Mercy is made clear in this verse: It is because He is "the Loving," *al-Wadud*, in essence that mercy cannot but spring from His actions.

16. The term *peace-giving mercy* translates the single Arabic word *rawh*, which is deemed by most classical commentators to be synonymous with *rahma*, "mercy, compassion," but since it is also related to *raha* (meaning ease following constriction or grief), one needs to refer to its capacity to give peace as well as its function of bestowing mercy. See Asad, *The Message of the Qur'an*, vol. 3, p. 393, n. 88. See also 15:56, where "those who go astray" are mentioned as the only people who despair of divine Mercy; this shows that *kafirun* means here not so much disbelievers in the ordinary sense—a disbeliever by definition can have no hope in the mercy of a God in whom he does not believe—as one who is ignorant of the nature of God, having attempted to "cover over" (which is the literal meaning of *kafara*) or deny the truth inscribed in his heart, and thus straying from the normative disposition of human nature, of which unfailing trust is one key dimension.

7:199

Adhere to forgiveness, enjoin kindness, and avoid the ignorant.

8:29

O you who believe, if you are mindful of God, He will grant you discernment, and efface your sins, and forgive you. And God is of infinite grace.

8:61

And if they [your adversaries] incline towards peace, then incline towards it also, and trust in God.

11:90

Seek forgiveness from your Lord and turn to Him repentant: Truly my Lord is Merciful, Loving.[15]

12:87

[Jacob said to his sons:] . . . and do not despair of God's peace-giving mercy; truly, it is only disbelievers who despair of God's peace-giving mercy.[16]

17. The Prophet Muhammad uttered these words of Joseph when he conquered Mecca. His foes and erstwhile persecutors, the Meccan Quraysh, were fearful of the retaliation that the victorious Muslims might wreak upon them. In uttering these words and issuing a general amnesty, the Prophet made it clear that the Meccans were being forgiven their vicious crimes against individual Muslims prior to the migration *(hijra)* of the community to Medina, their driving of the Muslims into exile, as well as their relentless military campaigns against the nascent Muslim state. This refusal to give rein to revenge and hatred can be seen as flowing from the principle expressed in verse 5:8: "never let hatred of a people cause you to deal unjustly with them." Likewise, this magnanimity in victory, stemming from the principle of mercy taking precedence over wrath, expresses the efficacy of the principle: "Repel [evil] with that which is most beautiful in goodness, and then [it can happen that] your enemy will be like a dear friend" (41:34–35). Among the Meccans who converted to Islam after the conquest of Mecca, one finds, indeed, that die-hard enemies were transformed into "dear friends."

[The brothers of Joseph, upon realizing the vizier of Egypt is none other than their own brother, whom they had left for dead in the well, exclaimed:] Could it be, are you really Joseph? He said: I am Joseph and this [pointing to Benjamin] is my brother. God has indeed been gracious to us. . . . They said: By God, indeed God has favored you over us, and we were transgressors. He said: No reproach will be made against you today![17] May God forgive you. And He is the most Merciful of the merciful.

13:21–24

[Those of understanding] . . . persevere in seeking the Countenance of their Lord, observe their prayers, and spend—both secretly and openly—from that which We have bestowed on them; and they repel evil with goodness. Theirs will be the ultimate [heavenly] abode—Gardens of Eden which they enter, along with all the righteous among their forefathers and their spouses and their seed. Angels enter unto them from every gate [saying]: Peace be with you, for you have persevered. How blessed and excellent is the ultimate abode!

18. The phrase *at peace* here translates *tatma'innu*, which is a quality of soul compounded of both peace and certainty, indicating that supreme, imperturbable state of serenity that rests on absolute certainty of the ultimate nature of the Real, source of all peace, beauty, goodness, and beatitude.

19. This teaching on the removal of bitterness from the hearts of those who are about to enter Paradise is of extreme importance and subtlety, for it helps to resolve the paradox of pious, even saintly, individuals being in opposition to each other on earth—even with "bitterness" in their hearts towards one another—but all of them being nonetheless on the threshold of Paradise.

[God] . . . guides to Himself all those who turn to Him, those who believe and whose hearts are at peace through the remembrance of God: Is it not through the remembrance of God that hearts are at peace?[18]

14:34–36

And He gives you everything you ask of Him; and were you to count the graces of God, you could not number them. . . . And [remember] when Abraham said: "My Lord, make safe this land and preserve me and my offspring from worshipping idols. My Lord, they have indeed led many astray. But whoever follows me is with me, and as for those who disobey me—Thou art surely Forgiving, Merciful."

15:45–49

Truly, the pious will be amid Gardens and springs. [It is said to them]: Enter them in peace, in security. And We remove whatever bitterness they have in their breasts [so that they enter] as brothers,[19] raised aloft on couches. No weariness afflicts them there, nor will they be expelled. Declare unto My servants, that verily, I am the Forgiving, the Merciful.

20. The subtle relationship between creation, truth, and wisdom on the one hand, and forgiveness and beauty on the other, is to be noted in these two verses. It is as if knowledge of the innermost truth that infuses the spirit of creation and by which it is governed—right up to its consummation in "the Hour"—is itself a source of beautiful compassion: The more one knows the beauty and compassion inherent in the creation, and *a fortiori* in the Creator, the more one must conform inwardly to this beautiful compassion and practice it outwardly.

15:56

He [Abraham] said: "But who despairs of the mercy of his Lord save those who go astray?"

15:85–86

We created not the heavens and the earth and all that is between them except with the Truth, and indeed the Hour is surely coming. So forgive with a beautiful forgiveness. Truly, your Lord is the Wise Creator.[20]

16:125

Call unto the way of thy Lord with wisdom and beautiful exhortation, and hold discourse with them [the People of the Book, that is, Jews and Christians] in the finest manner.

16:126

If you respond [to any opposition], then respond in a proportionate manner, but if you bear [it] patiently, that is better. So be patient. You cannot be patient except by the grace of God.

21. As noted in the Introduction, this verse is of great significance as regards the entire meaning of judgment and places in a different light the meaning of God's "wrath" and hell. In the case of a sinner, the "wrath" of God and "sentence" of punishment meted out to the soul can be seen here as the soul's own "judgment" upon itself: The now fully awakened conscience of the soul, seeing by the light of eternal values in its resurrected state, knows what purification is needed. The soul sees clearly that "whatever good comes to you is from God, and whatever evil comes to you is from your own soul" (4:79). It is goodness, compassion, peace, and love that emanate from God to us; whatever else we experience is solely the result of our own deeds, attitudes, and dispositions.

17:13

And We have tied every man's augury to his own neck, and We shall bring forth for him on the Day of Judgment a book which he will find open wide. [It will be said to him:] Read your book. Your own soul suffices this day unto you as a reckoner.[21]

17:23–26

Your Lord has decreed that you worship none but Him, and that you be kind to your parents. If one of them or both of them attain old age with you, do not rebuke them with expressions of exasperation, nor repulse them, but speak with them in a reverent manner. And humbly spread over them wings of mercy, and pray: "My Lord, have mercy on them, for they cared for me when I was young." Your Lord is best aware of what is in your souls. If you are righteous—then He is indeed ever forgiving to those who turn [to Him]. And give your relatives their due, and the needy, and the wayfarer; but do not squander your means wastefully.

22. As noted in the Introduction, this quasi-equivalence between the supreme Name *Allah* and the Name *al-Rahman,* the Compassionate, is another confirmation of the principle that compassion manifests the very heart of the divine nature, which can thereby be more deeply appreciated as infinite love and overflowing beatitude.

23. Contrary to what Christians might have expected, the Annunciation of the Virgin Birth is found in the Koran. It is given here in a manner which stresses the merciful aspect of the miracle of Jesus' birth. The sending of every prophet participates in the central function of prophecy: to be a merciful revelation from the Absolute to the relative, such being the universal principle of all miracles. See 21:107 and the Introduction for discussion.

17:110

Say [O Prophet]: Call upon God or call upon
the Compassionate—whichever of these two
you call upon, unto Him belong the most
beautiful Names.[22]

19:16–21

And remember Mary in the Scripture: when
she had withdrawn from her people to a
chamber looking East, and had chosen to se-
clude herself from them. Then We sent unto
her Our Spirit and it assumed for her the like-
ness of a perfectly formed man. She said: "I
seek refuge in the Compassionate from you,
if you are God-fearing." He said: "I am but
a messenger of your Lord [to announce to
you] the bestowal upon you of a pure son."
She said: "How can I have a son, when no
man has touched me, and I have not been un-
chaste?" He said: "So shall it be, your Lord
says: This is easy for Me—We shall make of
him a revelation for mankind and a mercy
from Us, and it is a thing ordained."[23]

19:96

Truly, those who believe and do good works,
the Compassionate will grant them love.

24. It should be noted here that this verse—regarded by many commentators as the first one granting permission to the Muslims to fight back in self-defense against the polytheists of Mecca—relates the need to resort to self-defense directly to the principle of defending *all* places of worship. Fighting to defend believers and their places of worship is thus to be understood in essence as an act of compassion for the sake of peace, and in order to establish the conditions in which devotion can be performed. One is reminded here of Jesus forcefully whipping the money-lenders out of the Temple.

21:83

And [remember] Job, when he cried unto his Lord: "Adversity afflicts me! And Thou art the most Merciful of the merciful." And We heard his prayer and removed the adversity from which he suffered, and We restored to him his household, and the like thereof along with them, as a mercy from Us, and a remembrance for the devout.

21:107

We sent you not [O Prophet] save as a mercy for all the worlds.

22:39–41

Those who have been attacked are permitted [to fight back] for they have been wronged— and God is indeed able to give them victory —those who have been driven from their homes unjustly, only because they said: "Our Lord is God." And had God not repelled some men by means of others, then indeed cloisters and churches, synagogues and mosques—places wherein the Name of God is invoked in abundance—would assuredly have been destroyed.[24]

25. See also 13:22, above, and 41:34, below. The word we have rendered as "most beautiful goodness" is *ahsan,* the root of which is the same as that of *ihsan;* as noted in the Introduction, this word comprises both beauty and goodness; it is often simply translated as "better," "most fine," "most excellent," and so on, but one needs to bring out the idea of beauty inherent in the root of the word if one is to do justice to it.

26. This passage on God's acceptance of authentic repentance has been included here to stress the ever-present possibility of escape from the consequences of one's sins. The iron law of cause and effect is here subordinated to the infinite power of God's Mercy, which can manifest not just in the Hereafter in the form of forgiveness, but also in the herebelow, as transformative grace: When man turns in sincere repentance to God, then God turns, relenting, unto man, effacing his evil deeds and transforming them into good ones. The message of hope here is unmistakable: Human sins are relative; divine Mercy is absolute.

23:96

Repel evil with the most beautiful goodness. . . .[25]

25:63

The servants of the Compassionate are
they who walk upon the earth humbly, and
when the foolish address them, they answer:
"Peace!"

25:69

The punishment will be doubled for him [who
engages in polytheism or commits murder or
commits adultery] on the Day of Judgment,
and he will abide therein disdained—except
him who repents and believes and performs
righteous acts; as for such, God will trans-
form their evil acts into good ones. And God
is ever Forgiving, Merciful. And whoever repents and acts righteously, he verily repents to
God with true repentance.[26]

26:215

And [O Prophet] warn your near of kin; and
spread your wing [of kindness] over those believers who follow you; and if they disobey
you, say: "I am innocent of what they do"; and

trust in the Mighty, the Merciful, who sees
you when you stand [in prayer], and who sees
your bowing among those who make prostra-
tion. He, verily, is the Hearer, the Knower.

27:19

[Solomon said:] "My Lord, inspire me with
gratitude for the grace which Thou hast bestowed upon me, and upon my parents; and
inspire me to do good that shall be pleasing
unto Thee; and admit me, by Thy Mercy, into
the ranks of Thy virtuous servants."

30:21

And among His signs is this: He created for
you spouses from yourselves, that you might
find repose with them, and He established between you love and mercy. Truly herein are
signs for those who reflect.

27. The divine injunction to be grateful to God and to one's parents has a metaphysical resonance in addition to its obvious moral stress on the relationship between filial piety and religiosity, or piety as such: One's parents are the immediate physical source of one's existence, whereas God is the ultimate cause of all existence. One's natural gratitude and respect for one's parents should therefore be deepened by giving thanks and reverence to the absolute source of one's existence, and conversely, gratitude to God for the gift of life and all other blessings must comprise thanks to one's parents. Even if they err—as the rest of the verse continues—one has no right to be anything but polite, kind, and courteous to them. This is in accordance with verse 17:23.

28. Luqman is a figure around whom many legends evolved through the ages. Very little is known of him. He was popularly associated with Aesop. This chapter, number 31, is named after him. He was renowned for his wisdom.

And We have enjoined upon man concerning his parents—his mother bears him, through weakness upon weakness, and his weaning is for two years—give thanks to Me and to your parents. Unto Me is the journeying.²⁷ But if they try and force you to associate with Me things of which you have no knowledge, do not obey them. But keep their company in the world with all due propriety and kindness. . . .

31:17–19

[Luqman²⁸ said:] "My dear son! Perform due worship, and enjoin what is good and forbid what is bad; and be patient in the face of whatever might befall you. Truly, this goes to the heart of the matter. And do not turn your nose up at people, nor swagger around haughtily—for God has no love for arrogant boasters. Rather, be modest in your bearing, and lower your voice—truly, the ugliest of voices is the braying of the ass."

33:35

Truly, the men who submit [to God] and the women who submit, the men who believe and the women who believe, the men who obey

and the women who obey, the men who are
sincere and the women who are sincere, the
men who are patient and the women who
are patient, the men who are humble and the
women who are humble, the men who are
charitable and the women who are charitable,
the men who fast and the women who fast, the
chaste men and the chaste women, the men
who remember God much and the women
who remember—for them God has prepared
forgiveness and a tremendous reward.

33:41–44

O you who believe, remember God with
much remembrance, and glorify Him in the
morning and evening. He it is who blesses
you, as do His angels, that He may bring
you out of darkness into light; and He is ever
Merciful unto the believers. Their salutation
on the day they meet Him will be: Peace. And
He has indeed prepared for them a generous
recompense.

33:45–47

O Prophet, We have sent you as a witness; and
as a bearer of good tidings; and as a warner;
and as a summoner unto God, by His leave;

29. The Arabic here is *Shakur,* and is one of the Names of God, "the Grateful." The translators shy away from the literal meaning of this Arabic name—for fear of excessive anthropomorphism, one suspects. For example, Pickthall translates the word as "bountiful," Muhammad Asad renders the term "ever responsive to gratitude," and Abdel Haleem, coming closer to the literal meaning, uses "appreciative." There should be no problem translating this term literally as "grateful," inasmuch as the gratitude of humanity is itself but an expression of the archetype of gratitude, which must, like all positive qualities, be rooted in the divine nature. An answer to the question: To whom or for what can God be grateful? was once given by Dr. Martin Lings (d. 2005), a leading authority on Sufism: "He is grateful to Himself for His own Absolute, Infinite Perfection." This answer, needless to say, does not prevent one from asserting that God is also "appreciative" in relation to man's devotion and virtue.

30. The rhetorical question here is of great significance. It is as if one were being invited to contemplate a link of merciful necessity between God's creation "with Truth"—together with all the laws of nature, summed up in the beautiful harmony of the heavenly spheres— and His being both mighty, as Creator of this magnificent universe, *and* forgiving in relation to the whole of His creation. Just as natural law ordains that night "enwraps" day and day "enwraps" night, so the supernatural "Law," that of overflowing mercy, ordains that the Creator "enwraps" His creation with forgiveness and infinite mercy. It is to be noted also that the primary meaning of the word *ghaffar,* "forgiver," is to conceal, cover over: One sees more clearly the relationship between the natural "enwrapping" of day and night and the divine "covering over" of the sins of mankind.

and as an illuminating lamp. So give unto the
believers the good tidings that they will have
from God grace in overflowing abundance.

35:33

Gardens of Eden! They enter them wear-
ing armlets of gold and pearl, and their gar-
ments there are of silk. And they say: "God be
praised, He who has taken from us all grief;
truly, our Lord is Forgiving, Grateful;[29] He
who, by His infinite grace, has settled us in
the everlasting Abode, where we are afflicted
by neither toil nor fatigue."

39:5

He has created the heavens and the earth with
Truth. He enwraps night by day, and day by
night; and He has subjected the sun and the
moon to service, each coursing its way to an
appointed term. Is He not the Mighty, the
Forgiver?[30]

31. One can interpret in the light of this verse any other verse
    that appears to restrict the universal scope of divine for-
    giveness, such as the one that says that God forgives all
    sins except *shirk,* the sin of setting up "partners" with
    God. Although theologians may insist on overcoming
    the apparent contradiction by making *shirk* the excep-
    tion that proves the general rule, the Sufis uphold the
    universal principle without allowing for any exception
    whatsoever. Ibn Arabi, for example, ingeniously argues
    that the reason why God cannot forgive *shirk* is that
    there is nothing to forgive, for the putative "partners" to
    God do not exist!

39:53

O My servants, you who have been prodigal
to your detriment: Despair not of the mercy of
God. Truly God forgives all sins. Verily, He is
the Forgiving, the Merciful.[31]

40:7–9

Those [angels] who bear the Throne, and all
who are around it, hymn the praises of their
Lord and believe in Him, and seek forgiveness for those who believe, [saying:] "Our
Lord, Thou encompassest all things in mercy
and knowledge, so forgive those who re-
pent and follow Thy path, and protect them
from the pain of hell. Our Lord, admit them
into the Gardens of Eden which Thou hast
promised them, together with those of their
forefathers and spouses and descendants who
were righteous. Truly Thou art the Mighty,
the Wise. And protect them against all evil
deeds; those whom Thou protectest against
[the consequences of] evil deeds on that Day,
they are truly those unto whom Thou hast
been merciful. That is the supreme triumph."

32. This speech of the angels to those who believe and are virtuous can be understood on several levels. On one level, it can be appreciated as the result of the spiritual attraction generated by heartfelt faith suffused with virtue. To affirm the Absolute, and to be faithful to the Absolute, generates within one's soul that supreme "consolation" constituted by certainty of divine Mercy, of Paradise, of infinite beatitude. This certainty and the serenity it engenders can be seen as "guiding friends," both in this life and the next. The angels can thus be understood both microcosmically—as spiritual attitudes and dispositions—and macrocosmically, as absolutely real, objective spiritual beings, without one such "form" precluding the other.

40:40

Whoever commits an evil deed, he will be requited the like thereof, but whoever commits a good deed—whether male or female—and is a believer, will enter the Garden, where they will receive sustenance beyond all reckoning.

41:30

Truly, those who say: "Our Lord is God," and are then upright—upon such do the angels descend, saying: "Do not fear, and do not grieve, rather: rejoice in the good tidings of the Garden which you are promised. We are your guiding friends in the life of this world and in the Hereafter. For you [in that Garden] is all that your souls desire, and there you will have everything for which you ask: A gift of welcome from One who is Forgiving, Merciful."[32]

33. The relationship between patience and the blessings of good fortune should be seen in the light of verse 2:155, cited above. Just as God's Mercy and blessing are poured upon those who are patient in adversity, so, in this verse, one who responds to evil with goodness and beauty— thus responding in a manner truly "divine," for God's Mercy in the face of human sin is nothing other than responding to evil with goodness—is one upon whom God's blessings and Mercy are bestowed, such blessing being not only the consequence of patience, but also its cause: "Be patient. You cannot be patient except by the grace of God" (16:126). From one point of view, human effort responds to God's grace, referred to in this verse as a "call": "O you who believe, respond to God and the Messenger when He invites you to that which gives you life" (8:24); from the other, it is God's grace that responds to man's call: "I answer the prayer of the suppliant when he calls upon Me" (2:186).

34. God's remoteness and transcendence—expressed in terms of exaltation and tremendousness—are connected to the fact that all things in the heavens and earth "belong" to Him, and His intimacy and immanence— expressed in terms of forgiveness and mercy—are mysteriously figured against the backdrop of the immense pressure on "the heavens" generated by the angels' prayers for forgiveness for those on earth. It is as if one is being compelled to see the irresistible power that inheres in invoking the Mercy of God.

41:34–35

The good deed and the evil deed are not equal. Repel [evil] with that which is most beautiful in goodness, and then [it can happen that] your enemy will be like a dear friend. But none is granted [such a capacity to respond to evil] except those who are patient; and none is granted it except those who have been blessed with immense good fortune.[33]

42:4–5

Unto Him belongs all that is in the heavens and the earth; and He is the Exalted, the Tremendous. The heavens might almost be split asunder while the angels hymn the praise of their Lord and ask forgiveness for those on earth. Is God not the Forgiver, the Merciful?[34]

35. We are following Pickthall's translation of the word *Latif,* one of the Names of God, though one has to understand the "grace" in question in a very particular way. Abdel Haleem renders it as "most subtle"; Asad has "most kind." These diverse translations show that the concept in question, that of *lutf,* cannot be translated by a single word, as it expresses a synthesis of the following notions: grace, kindness, subtlety, intimacy, and immense power. One calls upon God using this Name only in cases of direst need. It is as if absolute power is unleashed by infinite kindness, a power that is irresistible by virtue of its absolute subtlety and thus all-pervasiveness.

36. Again, one is to "feel" the vibration of beauty inherent in the goodness *(husn)* being referred to. See the Introduction for further discussion.

42:19

God is gracious[35] unto His servants. He gives sustenance to whom He will. And He is the Strong, the Mighty.

42:22–23

You will see the unjust fearful of what they have earned, and it will surely befall them; but those who believe and act virtuously will be in the meadows of the Gardens. They have whatever they wish from their Lord; that is the super-abundant grace. This is what God declares to His servants who believe and act virtuously. Say [O Muhammad:] "I ask of you no reward, [I ask] only that you be loving towards the near of kin. And whoever does good, We shall increase it for him in goodness."[36] Truly, God is Forgiving, Grateful.

42:25–30

And He it is Who accepts repentance from His servants, and pardons evil deeds, and knows what you do, and responds to those who act virtuously, and gives them more of His overflowing bounty. . . . And He it is Who sends down the life-giving rain after they have despaired, and spreads far and

37. One observes here again a perfect balance between the requirements of justice and the prerogatives of mercy. On the plane of social order, the rights of justice—and hence proportionate requital—must be upheld, but there is a higher plane, where the spirit of forgiveness prevails, and the "reward" for which is "with God" Himself—it is this spirit that takes one to the "heart of the matter."

wide His Mercy. He is the Protecting Friend, the Praised. . . . Whatever affliction strikes you, it is the consequence of your own acts; and He pardons much.

42:36–43

Whatever you have been given is only a fleeting comfort for the life of this world; and that which is with God is better and more lasting, for those who believe and put their trust in their Lord: those who avoid the major sins and indecencies, and when they are angered, forgive; those who respond to their Lord, and observe the prayers, and whose affairs are decided by mutual consultation and who spend generously from what We have bestowed upon them; those who defend themselves when afflicted by oppression. And the requital of an evil deed is an evil one like it; but whoever forgives, and brings about peace, his reward is with God. Truly, God loves not the unjust. There is no cause to act against anyone who defends himself after being wronged. One has cause to act only against those who oppress people and act unjustly in the land, violating all rights. For them is a painful punishment. But for those who are patient and who forgive—[such virtues] go to the heart of the matter.[37]

38. We follow Arberry's translation of the Arabic *fa'sfah 'anhum* as "pardon them." Pickthall and Asad have "bear with them," but Abdel Haleem has "turn away from them"—and this accords with the way in which the majority of the classical commentators understand this phrase. These variations are due to the fact that the verb *safaha*, followed by *'anhum*, can mean either "pardon them" or "turn away from them." The former seems to be more logical in this context, given that it is difficult to conceive of the greeting "Peace" having much meaning when one has turned away from one's interlocutor. The instruction given here to the Prophet is also consistent with the description of the "servants of the Compassionate," who reply with the word "Peace" when they are addressed by "the foolish." Also in accord with this interpretation is the following unequivocal injunction: "Tell the believers to forgive those who place no hope in the days of God" (45:14).

43:88–89

And he [Muhammad] said, "O my Lord, these are people who do not believe." But pardon them and say: "Peace." For they will come to know.[38]

45:14

Tell the believers to forgive those who place no hope in the days of God—He will requite people for what they have done.

46:15

And We have enjoined upon man beautiful kindness. His mother struggles in bearing him, and struggles in giving birth to him—the bearing and weaning lasts for thirty months. When he has grown to maturity and attained forty years of age, he says: "My Lord, inspire me with gratitude for the grace which Thou hast bestowed upon me, and upon my parents; and inspire me to do good that shall be pleasing unto Thee; and make wholesome for me my offspring. Verily I have turned unto Thee repentant, and I am among those who submit in peace [to Thee]." Those are they from whom We accept the most beautiful of their deeds, and We overlook their evil deeds. [They are among] the people of Paradise—[thus is fulfilled] the true promise made unto them.

39. This "victory" refers in the first instance to the Treaty of Hudaybiyya (628), the outward terms of which were by no means seen by the Muslims as a victory. But the peace obtained by this treaty was in fact the seed of the victory that was manifested in the bloodless and entirely peaceful conquest of Mecca two years later, for it was during this period that peaceful conversion continued at such a pace that, when the treaty was broken by the Quraysh and the Muslims marched on Mecca, the overwhelming numbers of the Muslim army compelled the Quraysh to surrender without a struggle.

40. One reading of the "sins" of the Prophet—for it is the Prophet being addressed here, second person singular —is based on the Arabic rhetorical device of *ta'rid*, or allusion, one form of which is synecdoche: naming the whole by means of a part. Thus the Prophet here stands for his community, all of whose sins—those of the past and those yet to come—are forgiven. A typically Sufi interpretation continues by stressing that the Prophet's "community" is the whole of creation, since he was sent by God as "a mercy for all the worlds" (21:107), and not just for all Muslims. Thus, to the all-embracing temporal scope of forgiveness of sins, past and future, is added an all-encompassing spatial dimension: No part of creation can be excluded from the Prophet's "community."

We have assuredly given you a clear victory,[39] that God may forgive you your sins,[40] those of the past and those to come, and that He may perfect His grace upon you, and guide you upon a straight path, and that God may assist you with a mighty assistance—He it is who sent down the Spirit of Peace into the hearts of the believers that they may increase in faith upon their faith. . . . That He may bring the believing men and the believing women into Gardens that are watered by flowing rivers, wherein they shall dwell immortal, and that He may remit from them their evil deeds. That is the supreme triumph in the sight of God.

49:9–10

If two groups among the believers fall to fighting, then make peace between them. And if one violates the rights of the other, then fight the violators until they return to the commands of God; and if they do so, then make peace between the two parties with justice and fairness. Truly, God loves the just. The believers are indeed brothers, so make peace between your brethren, and be mindful of God, so that you be granted mercy.

49:13

O mankind, We have indeed created you male and female, and have made you nations and tribes, so that you might know one another. Truly, the noblest of you, in the sight of God, is the most pious of you. Truly, God is Knower, Aware.

50:31–35

And the Garden is brought nigh for those who were pious, no longer distant. [It is said:] "This is what you were promised, for every one of you who was penitent and mindful, who held in reverential awe the Compassionate, despite being unseen, and who comes [to Him] with a contrite heart. Enter it in peace. This is the Day heralding immortality." Therein they have all that they desire, and with Us there is yet more.

41. It is also to be noted here that the requital of evil action is identical with that action itself. In other words, the very performance of the evil action is its own punishment already, here and now, however much the veils of the herebelow, objectively and subjectively, obscure this fact. In the Hereafter, the "punishment" already constituted in seed form by the act—the foreshadowing of the repercussion generated within the conscience of the awakened soul—will be clearly seen and painfully experienced. However, what is of greater import here is the description of the reward for beautiful goodness. We have here yet another affirmation of the incommensurability between good and evil in the eyes of God: evil is requited only with itself, while beautiful virtue—*ihsan*—is rewarded with its own intensification and raised up to its highest pitch of sublime exaltation, being at one with the very nature of the divine reality.

Truly, the pious will be in Gardens with springs, receiving that which is given them by their Lord; for they had been virtuous before: sleeping but little at night, and before first light seeking forgiveness; and in their wealth, the beggars and the deprived had a rightful share. And in the earth are signs for those whose faith is profound—and in yourselves: can you not see?

53:31–32

Unto God belongs all that is in the heavens and the earth. He will requite those who do evil with what they have done, and reward those who acted with beautiful goodness with the most beautiful goodness.[41] Those who avoid the major sins and indecencies—except what is done unintentionally—[for them] your Lord's forgiveness is vast. He is aware of you from when He created you from the earth and when you were hidden in the wombs of your mothers. So do not ascribe purity to yourselves. He is aware of the pious.

42. Most of the classical commentators say that *najm* here refers to plants, although it also means "star(s)."

43. It is not just the creativity of the Compassionate that is to be noted here, but also the fact that the "measure" of things is determined by this quality of God, even though one might have expected the divine quality of justice to be stressed here. One is enjoined to be just in upholding the measure of all things, but this measure is itself fashioned by the compassion at the creative source of all things.

55:1–9

The Compassionate has taught the Koran, created man, taught him speech. The sun and the moon are in harmony; and the plants[42] and the trees prostrate, and the sky He has raised aloft, and He has established the measure [of all things], so that you do not violate this measure, but uphold it with justice, without falling short of it.[43]

56:10–11, 25–26

And the foremost, they are the foremost: It is they who are brought nigh, in Gardens of bliss. . . . There they hear no vain talk nor incitement to evil; only the utterance: "Peace, Peace."

57:21

Race one with another for forgiveness from your Lord, and a Garden whose breadth is that of the heavens and the earth, which is prepared for those who believe in God and His messengers. Such is the bountiful grace of God, which He bestows upon whom He will; and God is of tremendous overflowing grace.

44. This translates the divine Name *al-Mu'min*. See discussion of the terms *iman* and *mu'min* in the Introduction.

45. It is to be noted that all the divine Names are designated as "most beautiful" *(husna)*, not just those that more overtly express the beautiful, loving, compassionate aspects of the divine nature.

57:27

. . . And We caused Jesus, son of Mary, to follow, and gave him the Gospel, and placed kindness and mercy in the hearts of those who followed him.

59:22–24

He is God, apart from Whom there is no other deity: the Knower of the Invisible and the visible. He is the Compassionate, the Merciful. He is God, apart from Whom there is no other deity: the King, the Holy, Peace, Granter of Security,[44] the Guardian, the Almighty, the Compeller, the Superb—glorified be God above all that they associate [with Him]. He is God, the Creator, the Maker, the Fashioner. His are the most beautiful Names. All that is in the heavens and the earth glorifies Him; and He is the Mighty, the Wise.[45]

60:4–8

You have a beautiful example in Abraham and those with him, when they told their people: "We disown you and what you worship apart from God. We renounce you. There has verily arisen between us opposition and hatred, which will endure until you believe only in

God"—except that Abraham said to his father: "I will ask forgiveness for you, though I have nothing for you in the [power of] God." [They said:] "Our Lord, in Thee we put our trust, and unto Thee we turn repentant, and to Thee is the journeying. Our Lord, do not make us a temptation for those who disbelieve, and forgive us, our Lord—Thou, Thou alone, are the Mighty, the Wise."

In them [Abraham and his companions] you have a beautiful example, [one to be followed by] those who place their hope in God and the Last Day. And even if they turn away, God is [nonetheless] the Independent, the Praised.

It is possible that God will ordain love between you and your enemies. God is Almighty. And God is Forgiving, Merciful. God does not forbid you from showing kindness and dealing justly with those who have not fought against you, nor driven you from your homes. Truly, God loves the just.

64:14

O you who believe, from among your wives and your children are opponents, so beware of them. But if you pardon and forbear and

46. See note 9 regarding the word *halim*.

forgive—then assuredly God is Forgiving, Merciful. Your wealth and your children are but a source of temptation, whereas with God is a tremendous reward. So be as mindful of God as you are able, and listen and obey, and spend generously: that is better for your souls. And whoever be saved from the avarice of his soul—such are the truly successful. If you lend God a beautiful loan, He will double it [in repayment] for you, and He will forgive you; for God is Grateful, Gentle.[46]

73:20

Verily, your Lord knows [O Muhammad] that you stand in prayer well-nigh two-thirds of the night, and [sometimes] half of the night, or a third of it—as do a group of those with you. God determines the measure of the night and the day. He knows that you cannot keep pace with it, therefore He has relented unto you. So recite as much of the Koran as is easy for you. He knows that some among you are sick, some who journey in the land seeking God's bounty, and some who are struggling in God's cause—so recite as much of it as is easy, and pay the alms, and lend unto God a beautiful loan. Whatever good you have accomplished for yourselves in advance, you will find it with

47. The juxtaposition between God's wrath and His Mercy in this passage is an illustration of the principle referred to in the Introduction, the combination of the "promise" and the "threat." God does "whatever He will," but given the fact that He is above all else "the Forgiving, the Loving," as has been made abundantly clear from the passages quoted, one is perfectly justified in asserting that there is nothing arbitrary about the will of God, such that His inscrutable will be deemed capable of casting good souls into hell and bad ones into heaven. As the Koran asks rhetorically: "Shall We treat those who believe and act virtuously as We treat those who spread corruption on earth? Or shall We treat the pious as We would treat the wicked?" (38:28). Thus, the saying "He does whatever He will" must be understood in the light of the principle that He can only *do* what He *is* by nature: just and compassionate. We have seen that He has "prescribed mercy" for Himself, because He is the very essence of mercy and love. Goodness and mercy, then, flow from the nature of God, whereas evil and "punishment" derive solely from our own actions.

God; but it will be better and an infinitely greater recompense [than that which your action merits]. And ask forgiveness of God; verily, God is Forgiving, Merciful.

76:5–11

Verily shall the pious drink of a cup that is flavored with camphor, flavored from a fountain from which the slaves of God drink [directly], gushing it forth in copious draughts. They fulfill their vows, and fear a day whose woes are widespread; and they feed the poor, the orphan, and the captive, for the love of God [saying]: "We feed you only for the sake of God. We seek neither reward nor thanks from you. Truly, we fear that Day of our Lord—a Day of distress and anguish." So God protected them against the woe of that Day, and has granted them radiance and joy. . . .

85:12–16

Truly, the punishment of your Lord is severe. Truly, He it is who originates [all things], then brings [them] back [to Himself]. And He is the Forgiving, the Loving; Lord of the Glorious Throne; He does whatever He will.[47]

48. The word here is *husna*, which should always be understood alongside the notion of beauty *(husn)*, as pointed out earlier.

89:27–30

O soul at peace in certainty! Return to your
Lord, well-pleased and well-pleasing: enter
among my servants; enter my Paradise.

90:4–17

We have indeed created man to strive and toil.
Does he think that none has power over him?
He says, "I have squandered vast wealth"—
does he think that none watches over him?
Have We not given him two eyes, and a tongue,
and two lips; and did We not show him the
two clear ways [of good and evil]? But he has
not attempted the steep path—and what will
convey unto you what the steep path is? It is
to free a slave, to feed when hungry an orphan
near of kin, or a poor person in misery; and
to be of those who believe, and exhort one
another to patience, and exhort one another
to compassion.

92:5–11

Truly your efforts are diverse. As for him
who gives generously and is pious, and who
confirms virtue,[48] We surely will smooth his
way unto ease. But as for him who is miser-
ly and self-satisfied, and who denies virtue,

49. One should note here that the "most pious" is generous
and compassionate and knows that the one who most
benefits from his generosity is himself, in that he "puri-
fies" himself of the sins of selfishness and miserliness.
When he gives only for the sake of God, and not for the
sake of any reward from those upon whom he bestows
his wealth, or from anybody else—including his own
ego, in the form of complacency or self-satisfaction—the
result is imperturbable contentment. In this connection,
see verses 76:5–11.

We surely will smooth his way unto adversity. His wealth will be of no avail when he perishes.

92:17–21

Far removed from it [the Fire] will be the most pious, he who gives his wealth that he may purify himself; none has any favor that might reward him—he seeks only the Countenance of His Lord Most High. He verily will be content.[49]

93:6–11

Did He not find you an orphan, and shelter you?

And did He not find you wandering, and guide you?

And did He not find you needy, and enrich you?

So do not oppress the orphan, and do not drive away the beggar: and of the graces of God be your discourse.

50. In this final extract, we see stress placed on the central
    aim of religion, and the meaning of triumph in Koranic
    terms: It is, on the one hand, the glorification of God by
    man, and on the other, the forgiveness of man by God.

107:1–7

Have you seen him who belies religion? The one who repels the orphan, and urges not the feeding of the needy? So woe be to those who pray, but are heedless of their prayers! Those who make a pretense [of piety], and withhold acts of kindness.

110:1–3

When the help of God and the Triumph come; and you see mankind entering the religion of God in droves—then hymn the praises of your Lord, and pray for forgiveness: He is ever turning [to you] in forgiveness.[50]

Reza Shah-Kazemi is a widely published scholar and translator and the author of a number of books, including *Paths to Transcendence: According to Shankara, Ibn Arabi and Meister Eckhart; Justice and Remembrance: An Introduction to the Spirituality of Imam Ali;* and *The Other in the Light of the One: The Universality of the Qur'an and Interfaith Dialogue.* In 1994 Shah-Kazemi co-launched the journal *Islamic World Report,* a publishing company producing works that combine objective scholarly analysis of the contemporary Muslim world with an understanding of deeper cultural and spiritual principles. From 1997 to 1999 he served as a consultant to the Institute for Policy Research (IKD) in Kuala Lumpur, Malaysia, a political-cultural think tank, and as the general editor of the IKD Monograph Series, commissioning over twenty monographs in a variety of subject areas. He is currently a research associate at the Institute of Ismaili Studies, a trustee of the Matheson Trust, founding trustee and senior fellow of Alam al-Khayal, Lahore, fellow of the Royal Aal al-Bayt Institute, Amman, and a contributor to the BBC World Service program *Pause for Thought.*